D0239574

For Richard, Bea and Benj, with all my love.

Special thanks to Vanessa Kerner and Annie McQueen

First published in 2013 by Little Boo Publishing

ISBN: 978-0-9926167-0-0

From the author of **Tell Me About Heaven, Grandpa Rabbit!**
winner of a **Gold Prima Baby Award.**

little boo publishing

Bea gives up her Dummy

Written by **Jenny Album**   Illustrated by **Claire Keay**

little boo publishing

Bea had a dummy,
which she used ALL the time.

She used it in the day when she played…

She used it in the night when
she went to sleep.

And sometimes, she even
used it in the bath!

Then, one day, Mummy said, "Bea – you're far too old to use a dummy now. They're for little babies, not children as old as you."

"Also, dummies make your teeth stick out, so if you're not careful, you might start to look like a bunny rabbit."

Bea imagined what she would look like as a bunny rabbit – and she didn't like it very much.

Also, it was true what Mummy had said, she *was* the only one of her friends who still used a dummy.

"So what shall I do Mummy?" asked Bea.
"Give them to the Dummy Fairy of course!"
Mummy replied.

So the next day Bea and Mummy went round the
house and collected up all of her dummies.

They found a dummy at the bottom
of the toybox…

They found a dummy
under the sofa cushions…

They even found a dummy
underneath the piano.
(It was very dusty.)

That night Bea put all the dummies in a big brown envelope and left it outside her bedroom door.

Mummy told Bea that if she was a good girl
and went straight to sleep with a smile on
her face, she might receive something special
from the Dummy Fairy the next day.

So, with a happy little smile Bea drifted off to sleep.

Later that night, Bea woke up to see a tiny fairy
sitting on her lampshade.

"Hello," said the fairy, "I'm the Dummy Fairy, and I've come to take all of your dummies off to Fairyland."

"Why?" said Bea.

"Well," she replied, "we fairies have lots of uses for dummies…"

"Sometimes we use them as boats
to sail down the river."

"And the fairy children use them as
roundabouts to spin round and round
in the fairy playground."

"And when the weather's really bad in Fairyland, some fairies use them as umbrellas to shelter from the rain."

"Wow!" said Bea. "I didn't know that!"

Then she paused. "But Dummy Fairy…" she said. "I know the fairies really need my dummies, and I really do want them to have them. But…er…I still *really* want my dummy too!"

Gently the Dummy Fairy said, "Don't worry Bea, every time you start to miss your dummy, just think very hard about something you love to eat. If you do, I will magically make you *taste* that special thing in your mouth."

Then she waved her magic wand and
Bea went straight to sleep.

When she woke up, the envelope outside her door had gone. And in its place was a little present from the Dummy Fairy!

Bea was very happy.

That day, Bea didn't really miss her dummy at all.
But that night, when she went to bed, she did a bit.

So as she lay there, Bea decided to think very hard
about honey on hot buttered toast.

And guess what? Suddenly she could actually
taste the honey in her mouth.

The next night when she missed her
dummy she thought about thick, creamy
banana milkshake!

And the next night, she thought of...well she
didn't really think of anything very much really...
she just fell straight to sleep.

In the corner of the room a little fairy smiled
and waved goodbye.

Her magic was done…